25TH ANNIVERSARY EDITION

NO JUMPING ON THE BED!

TEDD ARNOLD

Dial Books for Young Readers
an imprint of Penguin Group (USA) Inc.

DIAL BOOKS FOR YOUNG READERS
A division of Penguin Young Readers Group
Published by The Penguin Group
Penguin Group (USA) Inc., 375 Hudson Street, New York, NY 10014, U.S.A.

Penguin Group (Canada), 90 Eglinton Avenue East, Suite 700, Toronto, Ontario, Canada M4P 2Y3 (a division of Pearson Penguin Canada Inc.)
• Penguin Books Ltd, 80 Strand, London WC2R ORL, England • Penguin Ireland, 25 St. Stephen's Green, Dublin 2, Ireland (a division of Penguin
Books Ltd) • Penguin Group (Australia), 250 Camberwell Road, Camberwell, Victoria 3124, Australia (a division of Pearson Australia Group
Pty Ltd) • Penguin Books India Pvt Ltd, 11 Community Centre, Panchsheel Park, New Delhi - 110 017, India • Penguin Group (NZ), 67 Apollo Drive,
Rosedale, Auckland 0632, New Zealand (a division of Pearson New Zealand Ltd) • Penguin Books (South Africa) (Pty) Ltd, 24 Sturdee Avenue,
Rosebank, Johannesburg 2196, South Africa • Penguin Books Ltd, Registered Offiices: 80 Strand, London WC2R ORL, England

The publisher does not have any control over and does not assume any responsibility
for author or third-party websites or their content.

Designed by Nancy R. Leo-Kelly
Text set in Coop Light
Manufactured in China on acid-free paper
1 3 5 7 9 10 8 6 4 2

Library of Congress Cataloging-in-Publication Data
Arnold, Tedd.
No jumping on the bed : 25th anniversary edition / by Tedd Arnold.
p.   cm.
Summary: Walter lives near the top floor of a tall apartment building, where one night his habit of jumping
on his bed leads to a tumultous fall through floor after floor, collecting occupants all the way down.
ISBN 978-0-8037-3563-7 (hardcover)
[1. Behavior—Fiction. 2. Jumping—Fiction. 3. Apartment houses—Fiction.
4. Bedtime—Fiction. 5. Humorous stories.] I. Title.
PZ7.A7379No 2012 [E]—dc23   2011021952

While updating the illustration style of this, my first book, to the more exaggerated cartoon stylings of my later work,
I felt it appropriate to also update my painting process. The images in this book were outlined in graphite on paper,
then scanned into digital files. The colors and textures were applied using Photoshop software.

For Walter, of course, and William too!

With love and gratitude to my wife, Carol, who made everything possible.

Thanks again to Paula Wiseman.

In remembrance of Peter Elek.

In his room near the top floor of a tall apartment building, Walter was getting ready for bed.

His father said, "If I told you once, I told you a million times: No jumping on the bed! One day it's going to crash right through the floor. Now lie down and go to sleep."

Walter plopped down on his pillow and squeezed his eyes closed. "Good night," said his father. He turned off the light and pulled the door almost shut. The room was dark and quiet . . .

except for a soft *thump, thump, thump* coming from the room above.

"That's Delbert upstairs," thought Walter.

He switched on his lamp. "If Delbert can jump on his bed, so can I!"

Walter jumped—higher and higher—until his hair brushed the ceiling. When he landed, the mattress creaked, the floor cracked, and his whole bed tipped up sideways. Then down through the floor went Walter, bed and all.

Walter's bedroom was directly above Miss Hattie's dining room. She was quite surprised when Walter landed in her spaghetti and meatballs.

"I was not expecting company for dinner," she mumbled with a mouthful of meatballs.

"*M-m-m,*" said Walter, "spaghetti is my favorite!" But he didn't have a chance to eat. His bed smashed through the table and kept right on crashing down through the floor.

Down and down fell Walter, Miss Hattie, the spaghetti, the bed, and all.

Mr. Matty didn't even notice a bed coming through his ceiling until a meatball bounced off his head. Miss Hattie landed in his lap and Walter splashed into his aquarium.

"I already had one bath tonight," said Walter. He wanted to watch the monsters on TV. But his bed crunched through the floor and took the TV with it.

Down and down fell Walter, Miss Hattie, Mr. Matty, the TV, the spaghetti, the bed, and all.

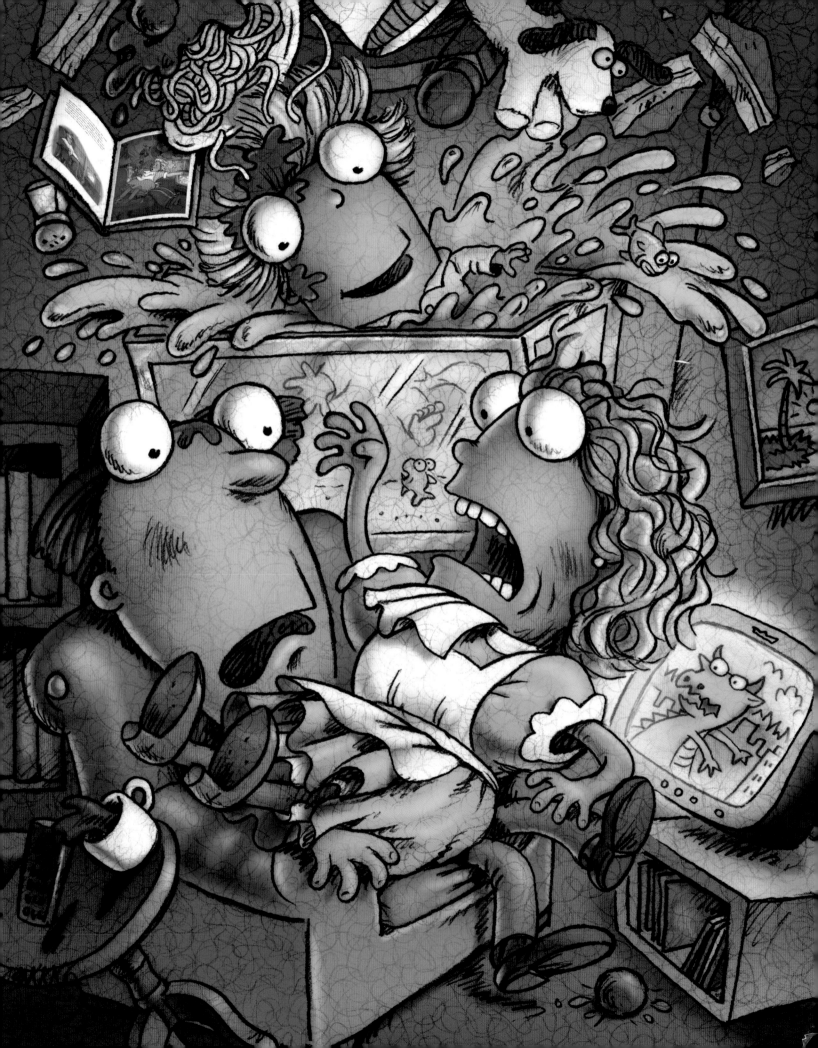

Walter's aunt Batty had just moved in. She was still unpacking when Miss Hattie, Mr. Matty, and a dripping wet Walter tumbled through the ceiling right into a box with her stamp collection.

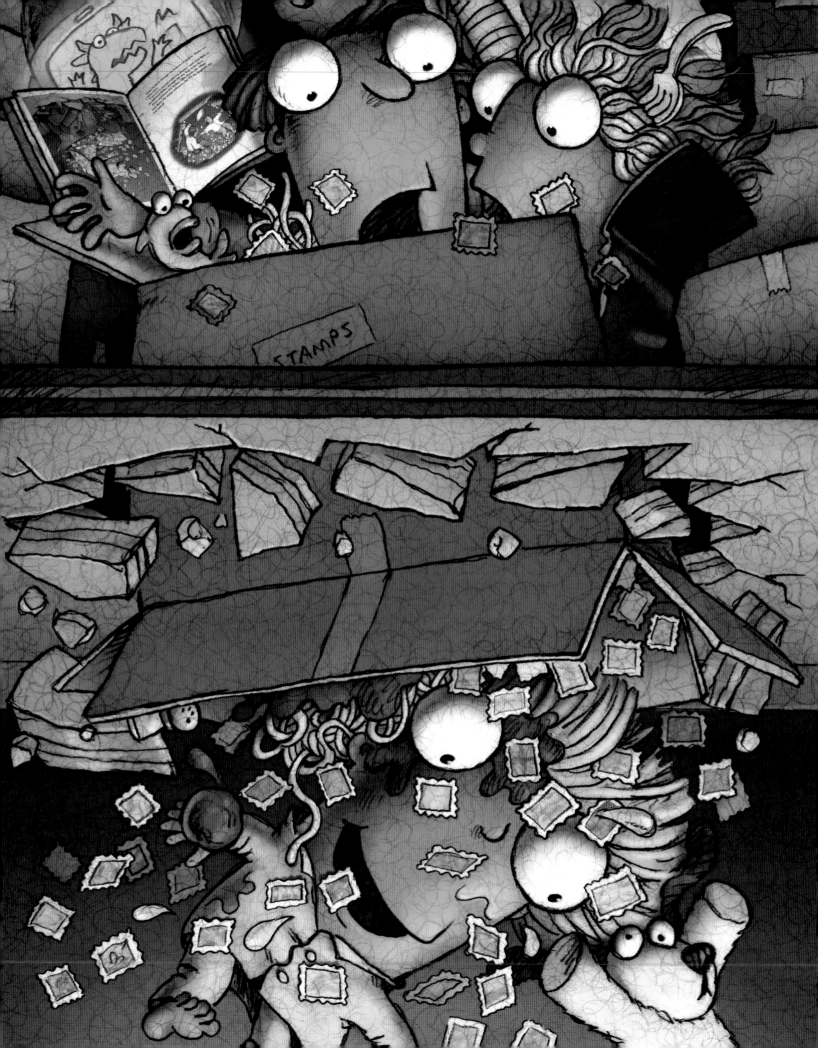

Walter burst through the bottom of the box and down through the floor. Aunt Batty soon followed.

Down and down fell Walter, Miss Hattie, Mr. Matty, Aunt Batty, the stamps, the TV, the spaghetti, the bed, and all.

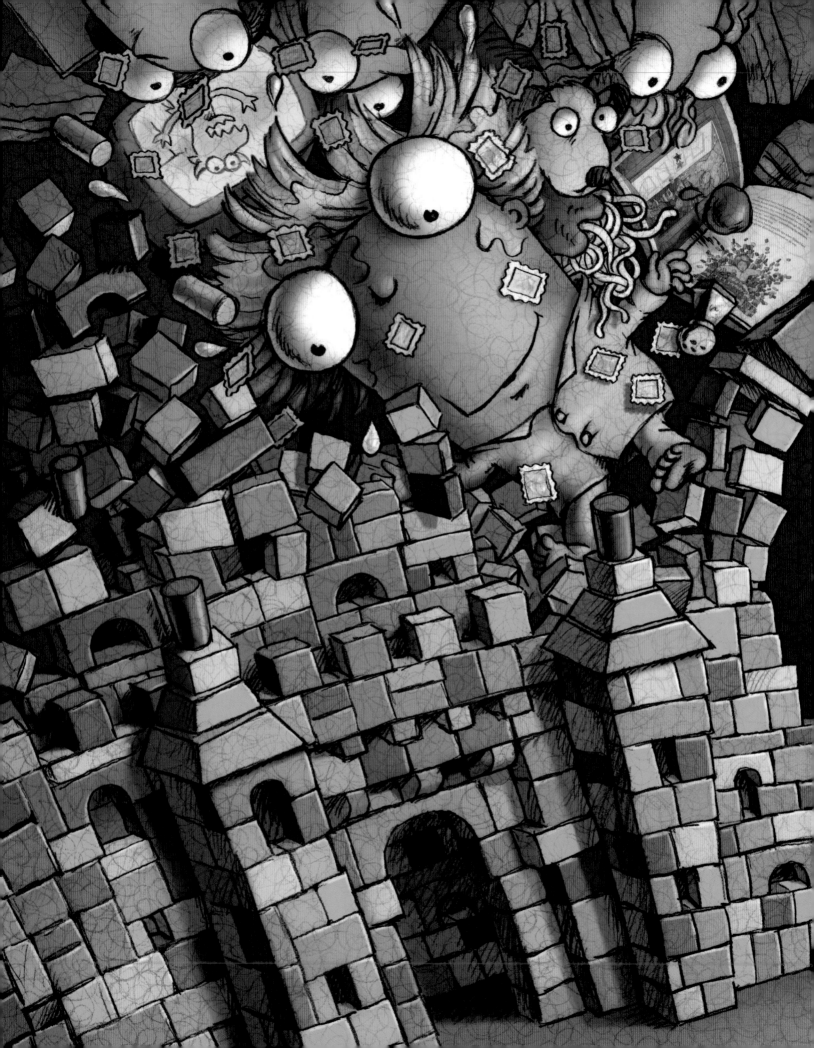

Patty and Natty had worked for days building a house of blocks. Afraid that Fatty Cat might knock it over, they shooed her out. Then the upstairs neighbors came through the ceiling.

"Excuse us," said Walter. "We won't be staying long." Then his bed crashed through the floor.

Down and down fell Walter, Miss Hattie, Mr. Matty, Aunt Batty, Patty, Natty, Fatty Cat, the blocks, the stamps, the TV, the spaghetti, the bed, and all.

The last thing Mr. Hanratty expected to see was a bed coming through his studio ceiling, followed by nearly everyone in the building. "If I knew you wanted to see my paintings," he said, "I would have tidied up a bit."

Then his floor caved in and everyone followed Walter's bed down through the hole.

Down and down fell Walter, Miss Hattie, Mr. Matty, Aunt Batty, Patty, Natty, Fatty Cat, Mr. Hanratty, cans of paint, the blocks, the stamps, the TV, the spaghetti, the bed, and all.

Maestro Ferlingatti and his string quartet were astonished by the colorful crowd that dropped in unannounced. "I love an audience!" he said.

But when paint
splattered everywhere,
the Maestro wished this
audience would leave.
And they did, taking
his string quartet
with them.

The Maestro's floor was also the basement ceiling. It was dark as midnight down there. Walter squeezed his eyes closed and fell through the darkness until he landed on something soft.

He opened his eyes. Everything was in its place! And outside the door his mother and father were talking quietly.

"Whew! No more jumping on the bed for me!" said Walter as he lay back down to sleep.

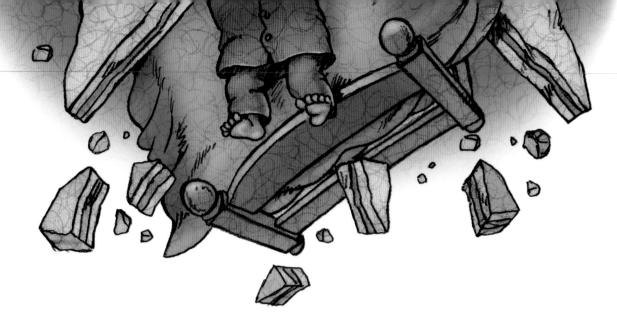

Suddenly he heard a creak, the ceiling cracked, and down
came Delbert, bed and all. Down and down fell Delbert . . .